...ho are just starting on the amazing
...ooks support both the acquisition of
...s.

The PURPLE LEVEL presents basic topics and objects using high
frequency words and simple language patterns.

The RED LEVEL presents familiar topics using common words
and repeating sentence patterns.

The BLUE LEVEL presents new ideas using a larger vocabulary
and varied sentence structure.

The YELLOW LEVEL presents more challenging ideas, a broad
vocabulary, and wide variety in sentence structure.

The GREEN LEVEL presents more complex ideas, an extended
vocabulary range, and expanded language structures.

The ORANGE LEVEL presents a wide range of ideas and concepts
using challenging vocabulary and complex language structures.

When sharing a book with your child, read in short stretches, pausing
often to talk about the pictures. Have your child turn the pages and
point to the pictures and familiar words. And be sure to reread favorite
stories or parts of stories.

There is no right or wrong way to share books with children. Find time
to read with your child, and pass on the legacy of literacy.

Adria F. Klein, Ph.D.
Professor Emeritus
California State University
San Bernardino, California

Editor: Christianne Jones
Designer: Amy Muehlenhardt
Page Production: Michelle Biedscheid
Art Director: Nathan Gassman
The illustrations in this book were created in watercolor and pencil.

Picture Window Books
1710 Roe Crest Drive
North Mankato, MN 56003
877-845-8392
www.capstonepub.com

Library of Congress Cataloging-in-Publication Data
Klein, Adria F. (Adria Fay), 1947-
Max goes to the doctor / by Adria F. Klein ; illustrated by Mernie Gallagher-Cole.
p. cm. — (Read-it! readers. The life of Max)
Summary: When it is time for his yearly checkup, Max goes to the doctor and gets
very good news.
ISBN-13: 978-1-4048-3680-8 (library binding)
ISBN-10: 1-4048-3680-2 (library binding)
ISBN-13: 978-1-4048-3686-0 (paperback)
ISBN-10: 1-4048-3686-1 (paperback)
[1. Physicians—Fiction. 2. Medical care—Fiction.] I. Gallagher-Cole, Mernie, ill.
II. Title.
PZ7.K678324Maq 2007
[E]—dc22   2007004051

Printed in the United States of America in North Mankato, Minnesota.
052017
010554R

Max
Goes to the Doctor

by Adria F. Klein
illustrated by Mernie Gallagher-Cole

Special thanks to our advisers for their expertise:

Adria F. Klein, Ph.D.
Professor Emeritus, California State University
San Bernardino, California

Susan Kesselring, M.A., Literacy Educator
Rosemount–Apple Valley–Eagan (Minnesota) School District

Picture Window Books
Minneapolis, Minnesota

Max is going to the doctor. It is time for his yearly checkup.

He wants to stay healthy.

The doctor checks how tall Max is.

Max has grown two inches. This
is good.

The doctor checks how much Max weighs.

Max has gained five pounds. This is good.

The doctor checks Max's blood pressure.

The doctor says it's like giving Max's arm a hug.

The doctor listens to Max's heart. It has a strong beat.

It beats eighty times in one minute.
This is good.

The doctor looks in Max's ears and eyes.

They both look healthy. This is good.

The doctor takes Max's temperature.

It is 98.6 degrees Fahrenheit. This is good.

The doctor gives Max two shots. The shots will help him stay healthy.

Max holds his mom's hand. He does not cry.

The doctor gives Max a sticker for
being brave.

Max had a great checkup. He is
very healthy.

WAIT!

DON'T CLOSE THE BOOK!

THERE'S MORE!

capstone **kids** .com

FIND MORE:

Games & Puzzles
Heroes & Villains
Authors & Illustrators

AT...

www.CAPSTONEKIDS.com

STILL WANT MORE?

Find cool websites and more books like this one at www.FACTHOUND.com.
Just type in the BOOK ID: 1404836802 and you're ready to go!

5